The Deer Watch

Pat Lowery Collins

illustrated by David Slonim

CANDLEWICK PRESS

It was another summer
in the house
that smelled like old trees

and where
the seagulls on the roof
believed they owned the place.

I didn't mind their noise,
because we were here
to look for deer.

It was the year my dad had promised

that I'd get to see

a doe or buck at last.

And so we planned

to get up early the next day.

As soon as there were

pink streaks in the morning sky,

we headed out.

In the dunes

the sand slipped underneath our feet

and made it hard to climb up to the top.

Everything below us

looked so small.

No speck of deer,

just flecks of gull,

a buoy like a painted cork,

a boat with a moth-wing sail.

No deer at all.

Next we looked
into the marsh grass,
where the deer come down
to drink or take a bath
before most people are awake.

We saw a red-winged blackbird
and one tall white shaggy bird,
its neck a question mark.

"Egret," said my dad.

On the road,

a bulldozer was moving

like a giant snail. It growled and sputtered

so we couldn't hear the birds.

The hammering and drilling

got so loud I had to hold my ears.

A workman told us

how a doe had come here

searching for the deer corn

that the hunters left

and how the crew had scared her off.

No deer here now, for sure!

We had to walk and walk

to find a green stretch

open to the sky. There

was a pond, a shiny mirror

full of trees all upside down

and water lilies right side up.

"Conservation land," said Dad, and told

how all the land for miles around

looked like this once.

The fields were dotted with bright wildflowers

and scrub pine that the deer could scratch against.

I knew they'd like it here.

I started pushing through the brush,
but then Dad stopped me and we stood
all quiet for a while until
I said, "There's nothing moving."

And Dad said it just seemed that way,
how baby birds were opening their beaks
while little foxes tussled in their dens
and mother squirrels went scavenging for food.

I squinted to look harder for the animals
my dad had talked about. I hoped
they wouldn't frighten off the deer.
My feet began to dance.
I swatted at a fly.
My throat was dry as sand.

Dad told how when

there weren't so many folks around

he'd seen a silver fox in this same spot

and how there'd soon be blueberries

that we could pick, enough to make a pie.

But it wasn't blueberries or foxes

that we'd come to find,

and even though this waiting was so hard

I knew we had to do it for that deer.

I hopped from one foot to the next

until I scared two rabbits off

and had to shut my eyes

to make my feet stay still.

Then all at once
we noticed something moving
through the bushes. Branches
swiveled side to side.

"Hey, look," I whispered
just before I sneezed
and one fat pheasant
that we hadn't seen
rose up into the air.

"I'll bet that bird will
tell the deer to stay away," I wailed.

"Then we'll go someplace
where they won't expect us," said my dad.

The sky was changing fast,
with yellow patches fading
into purple clouds.

The wind was cooler; darkness
fell like separate shadows
where the sun had shone before.

"Should we go back?" I asked
just as the lightning cracked
and thunder came so close
I grabbed Dad's hand.
The clouds dumped instant puddles,
drenched everything around.
The rain was warm. We turned our faces to it
and stuck out our tongues.

But then it stopped, as quick as it had come.
Do deer go out and drink the rain,
or do they hide away somewhere and wait?

Still dripping, we continued on
till Dad stood still.
"Look over there!" he said,
so softly that I almost didn't hear him,
and I didn't see a thing.

"Over where I'm pointing,
but don't move."

I held my breath until it burned my chest,
and I could just make out a white and pointy flag
with one beside it. They both twitched.

"Don't say a word," Dad said.

And then I saw her

stepping from the shadows,
and she looked at me — at me —
then leaped into the air.
The little flags bounced, too,
and I could see they were the tails
of two small deer.

"A doe and her two fawns," I said
as quietly as I could while trying
desperately to keep the three in sight
until they disappeared
into their green world.

The long walk home

along the stream,

past conservation land,

by all the houses being built,

then through the marsh

and over dunes,

I tried to think how I could see

that doe and her two fawns again.

There had to be a way.

When Mom came out,
I ran to tell her all about the doe
and how those twins had twitchy tails.

"You're such a lucky boy," she said.

But I couldn't seem to tell the rest,

so deep inside me that I knew

the memory would never leave —

the way those deer had suddenly appeared,

the way they'd quickly run away —

as if they'd come from nowhere

like Dad said,

or as if

our two worlds crossed

for just a magic while.

To Ellis James and Jennifer

P. L. C.

∼

For Dad

With special thanks to Brooks, Sue, and Matthew Parker

D. S.

First edition 2013

Library of Congress Catalog Card Number 2012942667

ISBN 978-0-7636-4890-9

13 14 15 16 17 18 LEO 10 9 8 7 6 5 4 3 2 1

Printed in Heshan, Guangdong, China

This book was typeset in ITC Cergio.
The illustrations were done in oil on linen.

Candlewick Press
99 Dover Street
Somerville, Massachusetts 02144

visit us at www.candlewick.com